Haunted house horror!

Katie slumped back on a stair. "I can't believe this is happening!" she said. "I can't believe Lester is missing!"

"Don't look now," George said. "But someone *else* is missing."

"Who?" Mari asked.

"Bess!" George replied.

"Bess?" Nancy gasped.

Her eyes darted around for her best friend. But George was right. Bess was gone!

The Nancy Drew Notebooks

Available from Simon & Schuster

THE
NANCY DREW
NOTEBOOKS®

#50

The Scarytales Sleepover

CAROLYN KEENE
ILLUSTRATED BY JAN NAIMO JONES

Aladdin Paperbacks
New York London Toronto Sydney Singapore

First Aladdin Paperbacks edition October 2002

Copyright © 2002 by Simon & Schuster, Inc.

ALADDIN PAPERBACKS
An imprint of Simon & Schuster
Children's Publishing Division
1230 Avenue of the Americas
New York, NY 10020

The text of this book was set in Excelsior.

Printed in the United States of America
10 9 8 7 6 5 4 3 2 1

NANCY DREW, THE NANCY DREW NOTEBOOKS, and colophon
are registered trademarks of Simon & Schuster, Inc.

Library of Congress Control Number 2001097940

ISBN 0-7434-3768-3

The Scarytales Sleepover

1

Chillin' with Villains

Since when do parrots go to sleepovers?" eight-year-old Nancy Drew asked her friend Katie Zaleski.

"My cousin is visiting and he's allergic to feathers," Katie answered. "So Amara told me I could bring Lester to the party."

Katie sat in the backseat of the Drews' car. She held her pet parrot's cage on her lap.

"Row, row, row your boat!" Lester screeched. "Arrrk!"

"He's going to keep us up all night!" Nancy's best friend Bess Marvin groaned.

"It's a sleepover!" Nancy's other best friend, George Fayne, said. "We're supposed to stay up all night!"

1

Nancy smiled. She sat in the front seat between her friend Mari Cheng and the Drews' housekeeper, Hannah Gruen. Bess, George, and Katie sat in the backseat.

"All aboard the sleepover express!" Hannah announced as she started the car.

Hannah had been the Drews' housekeeper since Nancy was only three years old. Hannah cooked yummy meals for Nancy and made sure her clothes were neat and clean. But today Hannah was driving Nancy and her friends to Amara Shane's first sleepover.

Nancy had been to sleepovers before, but this one would be special.

Amara was having her sleepover at Scarytales—a big old house where the villains from all different fairy tales—like the wolf from "Little Red Riding Hood" and Captain Hook from *Peter Pan*—came to life.

Amara's aunt Ellen owned Scarytales. She lived there with her seven-year-old son, Ernest.

"I can't believe we're spending the night with fairy tale villains!" Bess said. She tugged at her blond ponytail. "Those parts of the stories always gave me goose bumps!"

"Amara told us it's more fun than scary," Nancy said. "She's been there so many times she knows exactly what will happen."

"Villains are the best!" George said, her dark eyes flashing. "What would Hansel and Gretel be without the witch?"

"Safe!" Bess shuddered.

Mari shook her head at Bess and George. "Are you two sure you're cousins?"

"Last we checked!" George joked. George's real name was Georgia. But hardly anyone called her that.

Hannah drove the car through River Heights. It was only six o'clock but the October night sky was already dark.

"What's that around your neck, Mari?" Hannah asked.

"A camera!" Mari said proudly. "It develops pictures in just a few seconds!"

"Great!" Nancy said. "You can take pictures of all the villains!"

"If they let you," Bess groaned.

Hannah slowed the car down. "Here it is," she announced. "Scarytales!"

3

Nancy leaned over Mari to look out the side window. She saw a big old house and a yard filled with brown leaves. In front of the house was a narrow creek and a wooden bridge.

"This place is spooked," Mari said in a hushed voice.

"It just *looks* spooked!" Nancy said.

"Check out the tower on the roof!" Bess gasped. "Towers mean bats!" she exclaimed.

"No bats," Katie said, shaking her head. "Just witches, pirates, and trolls."

Hannah parked the car on the street. She helped the girls unload their sleeping bags and backpacks. Most of them wore jeans, sneakers, and long-sleeve T-shirts. Bess wore black pants and a bright orange sweater. Crunching through the leaves, they carried their gear toward the house. Hannah held Katie's sleeping bag so she could carry Lester's cage.

"I guess we have to cross that bridge to get to the house," Nancy said.

"Not so fast!" came a gruff voice.

A short man with a long white beard crawled out from under the bridge. He

4

wore blue overalls, a yellow shirt, and a pointed red hat. Three people dressed as goats ran out after him.

"You have to pay the toll first!" the little man said, holding out his hand.

"Or go baaaaack!" a goat said.

Nancy giggled. It was the mean troll from "The Three Billy Goats Gruff."

"Well?" the troll said. He was so small that he looked Nancy straight in the eye. "Are you going to cough it up?"

"Sorry." Hannah smiled. "These girls don't get their allowances until Monday."

Katie put Lester's cage on the ground. She reached into her pocket. "But you can have some cinnamon gum," she said.

"Nah," the troll said. "Cinnamon makes me sneeze."

"How about a baseball card?" George asked. She pulled a card from her pocket.

"Baseball?" the troll cried. He rubbed his hands. "Now you're talking!"

"If you're such a fan," George said, tilting her curly head, "how come *you're* not watching the play-offs tonight?"

The troll didn't answer as he snatched the

baseball card. "You can cross now," he said.

"What a grouch!" Bess whispered.

"He was just pretending," Hannah said as they walked over the bridge.

"Wait!" Mari said. "I want to get a picture of the troll and the goats!"

Nancy, Mari, and George ran back to the middle of the bridge. They leaned over the rail. Nancy couldn't see the troll or the goats. But she could hear them.

"Who says I'm not watching the baseball game tonight?" a voice asked.

Nancy looked at Mari and George. It was the troll's gruff voice.

"I happen to have a little plan up my sleeve," the troll went on.

The goats began to laugh. "You are so baaaad!" one goat said.

"I think I'll pass on that picture," Mari said softly.

But Nancy was curious. "What plan do you think the troll was talking about?" she whispered to her friends.

George shrugged and sighed. "Villains. You just can't figure them out," she whispered back.

7

Nancy, George, and Mari ran back over the bridge to join the others. They walked across the yard toward the front door.

Suddenly a tall man dressed in a wolf costume jumped out from behind a tree. Over his costume was a flannel nightgown.

"Greetings!" he said. He tipped his nightcap. "Are you on your way to Grandma's house?"

Nancy decided to play along. "My!" She laughed. "What big teeth you have!"

The wolf reached behind the tree and pulled out a pizza box. "The better to eat mushroom and pepperoni pizza with!" he declared. "You *will* share some with me, won't you?"

"Pizza isn't good for wolves," Hannah joked. "Especially if they *wolf* it down."

Hannah borrowed Mari's camera to take a picture of the wolf and the girls. They posed on the doorstep.

"Say cheese!" Hannah called.

"Pepperoni!" the wolf called back.

Hannah took the picture. The wolf gave a little wave. Then he disappeared behind the tree again.

"Amara was right," Nancy said excitedly. "This place is a blast!"

The front door flew open. Amara stood in the doorway. "I hope you weren't scared of the big bad wolf!" She giggled.

Mari held up her instant picture. All of the girls were smiling and laughing. "Does this look like scared?" she asked.

Amara waved everyone through the door. "My first sleepover!" she said. "This is going to be soooo cool!"

"Have a good time," Hannah said. "I'll pick you all up in the morning."

After Hannah left, Amara turned to her guests. "You can leave your stuff in the hall," she said. "I'll take you up to the tower to meet my aunt."

The girls propped their bags against the wall. Katie took Lester out of his cage and perched him on her shoulder.

Then Amara led everyone up a long staircase. The stairs took them straight to the tower.

"Ta-daa!" Amara sang. "Check out my aunt's office!"

"Wow!" Nancy exclaimed. The room

looked like something out of a fairy tale. The dark blue wallpaper was covered with gold stars. Wind chimes hung over a large desk. Wands, colorful bottles, and magic books lined rows of shelves.

"Now where did that go?" a woman's voice piped up.

Nancy saw a tall pointed hat rise up from behind a desk. Slowly a woman dressed in a star-covered robe stood up.

"Oh, hi!" she said, surprised. "I'm Aunt Ellen. Welcome to Scarytales!"

"Did you lose something?" Bess asked.

"My crystal ball." Aunt Ellen sighed. "I can't seem to find it anywhere."

"Are you a real wizard?" Mari asked.

"No!" Aunt Ellen laughed. "But I like to think I have the magic touch."

Just then Nancy heard Bess scream. She turned and saw why. . . .

Fluttering over Bess's shoulder was a brown bat!

2

Fee-Fi-Fo-Run!

I hate bats!" Bess squealed.

"That's not a bat," Amara said angrily. "That's my cousin Ernest!"

Nancy looked closer. The bat was dangling from a string attached to a pole.

Holding the pole was a seven-year-old boy. He wore a baseball cap and a grin.

"Ernest Shane!" Aunt Ellen scolded. "You just scared Amara's guest!"

Ernest pouted. "I wouldn't be doing this scary stuff if I could just go to Amara's sleepover!" he said.

"I told you a zillion times!" Amara cried. "This sleepover is for girls only!"

"But you're going to be scared!" Ernest said. He flexed his scrawny muscles. "You need a big strong guy like me to protect you!"

"Thanks," Katie said. "But we can protect ourselves. Right, Lester?"

"Right on!" Lester squawked. "Arrk!"

Ernest's eyes lit up when he saw the parrot. "A parrot!" he gasped. "Way cool!"

Nancy smiled. She couldn't blame Ernest for wanting to join the sleepover.

"You can have some of our pizza if you'd like," Nancy suggested kindly.

"No thanks," Ernest said. "I have better things to do." He flung his rubber bat over his shoulder and left the tower.

"Sorry, girls." Aunt Ellen sighed. "But Ernest can be a bit lively."

"You mean pesty!" Amara muttered.

Aunt Ellen shook hands with all the girls and learned each of their names.

"Are you going to show us around the house?" Nancy asked. "And introduce us to the villains?"

"No, Nancy," Aunt Ellen said. She smiled. "The villains will find *you*!"

"Say cheese!" Mari said, quickly snapping a picture of Aunt Ellen.

Aunt Ellen rubbed her eyes from the flash. "Now, why don't you girls settle downstairs in the library?" she said. "Before your pizza gets cold."

Amara explained the house as they ran down the stairs.

"Aunt Ellen and Ernest live on the second floor," she said. "There's a storage room in the basement. But all the fun stuff happens on the main floor."

The girls reached the main floor and they had company—a woman with a huge warty nose.

"Have you seen Hansel and Gretel?" the witch asked. She licked her lips. "They're late . . . for dinner."

Nancy recognized the witch from "Hansel and Gretel." She wore a long black skirt, a scarf, and a tattered shawl.

"May I take your picture?" Mari asked.

"Only if you get my best side," the witch said. She turned her head sideways.

That nose can't be real, Nancy thought as Mari snapped the picture.

"Wicked witch!" Lester squawked from Katie's shoulder. "Wicked witch—arrrk!"

"Ahh!" the witch said. She leaned in close to Lester. "That's exactly what I need for my next brew: feather of parrot!"

Lester stretched his neck. He nipped the witch right on her nose!

"Owwww!" the witch yelled. She grabbed her nose. "No one pecks me on the wart and lives to squawk about it!"

The witch then spun around and huffed down the hall.

"She was just *pretending* to be mad, right?" Bess asked.

Amara shook her head slowly. "I never saw her pretend like that," she said.

"And I never saw such a big honker," Mari said as she pulled out the picture.

The girls followed Amara down a hallway and past doors.

Nancy stopped at a door covered with vines. "What's this?" she asked.

"See for yourself," Amara said. She grabbed the doorknob and opened the door.

The girls stepped inside a room filled with plastic plants, trees, and flowers. In the middle was a thick green pole covered with vines.

"That's the bean stalk!" Amara said proudly. "Like the one Jack climbed."

Nancy looked up the bean stalk. It led to a big hole in the ceiling.

"What's up there?" Nancy asked.

"Climb it and find out!" Amara said.

A narrow green ladder was attached to the bean stalk. George climbed first. The others followed.

"Up, up, and awaaaay!" Lester squawked from his perch on top of Katie's head.

One by one the girls scurried through the hole in the ceiling. Soon they were standing in a room filled with a giant table, a giant chair, even a giant pair of slippers on the floor!

"Welcome to the giant's house!" Amara announced.

"Hey, look!" Mari said. She pointed to a plate of giant cookies on the table.

"They're from my aunt Ellen," Amara said. She held up a note that read: HOPE YOUR SLEEPOVER IS HUGE! LOVE, AUNT ELLEN.

The girls grabbed cookies. Then—

"Fee-Fi-Fo-Fum!" a voice boomed. "I smell chocolate chip cookies—YUM!"

The sound of thunderous footsteps filled the room. "Uh-oh!" Katie giggled. "Here comes the giant."

Nancy's eyes grew big. The floor felt like it was trembling!

The girls laughed and shrieked as they scurried back down the bean stalk.

"That was fun, Amara," Nancy said.

Amara wasn't smiling. "I think I need some . . . pizza," she said in shaky voice.

Hmm, Nancy thought. *Maybe Amara is afraid of heights!*

The girls stopped in the hallway and grabbed their gear.

"Don't go into the library until I take a picture," Mari said.

Nancy and her friends posed between the library door and a potted plant.

"If I say cheese one more time I'll turn into a mouse!" George whispered.

Mari snapped the picture. Then everyone filed into the library.

"This room isn't scary at all," Nancy said with a smile. There was a crackling fire in the fireplace, soft leather furniture, and bookshelves filled with fairy-tale books.

"It may be a library," Amara said, "but you don't have to whisper."

The girls piled their gear in a corner. Katie put Lester back in his cage. She placed the cage on a small round table.

"Okay, gang," Amara said. She lifted the lid of a pizza box. "Let's pig out!"

But when Nancy looked at the pizza she gasped. Written with mushrooms was the word BEWARE!

"That's a joke, right?" George asked.

Amara didn't answer. She handed out paper plates and the girls began to eat.

"Mmm," Bess said. "For a creepy pizza it sure is yummy."

"You guys," Mari said slowly. "Wasn't there a fire in the fireplace?"

Nancy turned to the fireplace. The flames were out. But then all of a sudden they shot back up!

"Did you see that?" Bess squeaked.

Just then a book fell off the shelf. Then another! And another! And another!

The girls giggled and screamed. They jumped up and ran out of the library.

"Way cool!" George cried.

"I'll bet you've seen that a gazillion times, Amara!" Nancy said.

Amara's eyes were as wide as Frisbees. She shook her head slowly. "No," Amara said. "I *never* saw the books fall off the shelves. Or the fireplace go on and off. And I never felt the giant's footsteps either!"

Nancy stared at Amara. No wonder she looked so scared!

"Uh-oh," Mari said. "Maybe this place really *is* spooked!"

3

Library Crook

I think I want to go home!" Bess said as the girls stood in the hallway.

Nancy didn't want Bess to be scared. She didn't want her to go home either.

"This is Scarytales," Nancy said. "Weird things are supposed to happen."

"Not like this," Amara said with a shudder. "This stuff is all new to me!"

Nancy heard someone humming. She looked back and saw Aunt Ellen.

"Let's ask your aunt," Nancy said to Amara. "She'll tell us what's going on."

Nancy told Aunt Ellen about the fireplace, the tumbling books, and the giant footsteps. She looked surprised.

"Really?" Aunt Ellen asked. "I've never

seen those things either!"

"Y-y-you haven't?" Amara stammered.

"But I will look into it!" Aunt Ellen said. She scratched her forehead as she continued up the hall. "Now if I could just find my crystal ball!"

The girls looked at one another. Everyone except Bess began to laugh.

"This is too weird!" George said, smiling.

"Now I know why they call it Scarytales!" Katie said with a giggle.

"But how did all that stuff happen?" Amara wanted to know.

Nancy gave it a thought. "What if," she said, "someone is trying to scare us?"

"Who?" Amara asked.

"Someone who knows this house inside out," Nancy said. "Someone who knows how to make weird things happen."

"Let's find out who!" George said. She ran over to a mirror hanging on the wall. Written on its thick gold frame were the words MAGIC MIRROR.

"Mirror, mirror on the wall," George began to chant. "Who is scaring us—once and for all?"

The girls crowded in front of the mirror. Everyone giggled, until the mirror began to crack!

"Guess what?" Amara said slowly. "This never happened before either."

The girls stared at the mirror.

"That does it," Bess said. "I'm out of here."

"But you packed three pairs of pajamas!" George cried, waving her arms.

"Wait!" Nancy said. "There must be a way to find out who's doing all this."

"You mean as in another mystery, Detective Drew?" Mari asked, smiling.

Nancy smiled back. She loved solving mysteries. She even carried a blue detective notebook where she wrote down all of her suspects and clues. Sometimes she even used a magnifying glass!

"Sure," Nancy said. "Solving a mystery at a sleepover could be fun."

"Better than telling ghost stories!" Katie exclaimed.

George turned to her cousin. "Do you still want to go home, Bess?" she asked.

"Nope," Bess said, shaking her head.

"Because Nancy is going to solve the case?" Amara asked.

Bess nodded. "And because we didn't finish that yummy pizza!" she said.

The six friends laughed and gave each other high-fives.

"I'll get my notebook and my magnifying glass," Nancy said. "They're both in my backpack in the library."

"And I have my camera," Mari reminded everyone. "To take pictures of clues."

"I only packed my toothbrush," Katie sighed. "Bor-ring!"

Before going into the library, Nancy checked the mirror for clues. She found a tiny silver spider on the frame.

"Ew!" Bess gasped. "Is it real?"

"It looks like a sticker," Nancy said. She carefully picked at the sticker.

Mari leaned over Nancy's shoulder and snapped a picture. The flash made Nancy see spots.

"Let's go into the library now," Nancy said, rubbing her eyes.

One by one the girls filed into the library. Nancy was about to get her notebook when Katie let out a shriek.

"Ohmygosh!" Katie cried. "Lester isn't inside his cage—he's gone!"

Nancy glanced at the cage. The door was wide open. "Maybe he kicked the door open," she said. "He's done that before."

"No, I closed the latch!" Katie wailed. "I didn't want him to get at our pizza!"

"Say," George said slowly. "You don't suppose Lester was . . . parrot-napped?"

"Parrot-napped?" Katie cried.

"But we were right outside the library all this time," Nancy said. "We would have seen someone go in or out."

"And there are no other doors in the library," Amara added.

Nancy checked the window. It was locked shut from the inside. And she noticed something else. "The dust on the windowsill is pretty even," Nancy said. "That means no one climbed in or out of the window."

The girls called Lester as they searched the room. Nancy saw how worried Katie was when he didn't squawk back.

This isn't funny anymore, Nancy thought. *This is serious!*

"What do you think, Nancy?" George asked. "Who do you think took Lester?"

All eyes were on Nancy now.

"I think," Nancy said slowly, "the person who took Lester is the same person who's trying to scare us."

She pulled out her notebook and turned to a clean page. On it she wrote the words TRUTH OR SCARE? Underneath the title she began her list of suspects.

"Who would want to scare *us*?" Mari asked, wrinkling her nose.

"How about Ernest?" Nancy asked, thinking. "He was mad that he wasn't invited to the sleepover. He also told us we'd be scared—and that he had 'better things to do.'"

"And he probably knows this house inside out," George said. "He lives here!"

Nancy wrote down Ernest's name.

"How about that witch?" George asked. "We haven't seen her since Lester bit her nose."

"Nipped!" Katie corrected. "Lester does not bite."

"Hey!" Mari said excitedly. "Maybe there's a clue in my pictures."

Mari spread her pictures on the rug. Nancy checked them all out. Something in the group picture caught her eye.

"There's something red behind that plant," Nancy thought out loud.

Nancy grabbed her magnifying glass and placed it over the picture. The red object was tall and pointy. Nancy recognized it right away. "The troll's red hat!" Nancy said. "Maybe he was waiting to sneak into the library."

"We did hear the troll say that he had a plan up his sleeve," George said.

"Maybe the troll's plan was to scare us," Nancy said. "Then if we went home, he could watch the baseball game!"

"Sneaky troll!" Katie muttered.

Nancy added the troll to her suspect list. "Good work, Mari!" she said.

"Don't mention it." Mari smiled.

The girls searched the library for more clues. Nancy found another spider sticker on the mantel.

"There it is again," Nancy said.

"And again!" Katie said. She pointed to a spider sticker on the bookcase.

"I never saw those spiders before," Amara said. "Where did they come from?"

"Who cares?" Bess shuddered. "As long as they're not real."

Nancy sketched the spider in her notebook. Then she heard a deep snarling voice. It was coming from the hallway and it was singing:

"Blow the man down, maties! Blow the man down! Yo, ho, blow the man down!"

The girls bumped into each other as they tried to squeeze through the door.

Once in the hall, Nancy saw a man wearing a black cape and a red bandana around his head. His back was to the girls as he walked up the hall.

"Who's that?" Nancy asked Amara.

"It's Captain Hook from *Peter Pan*," Amara explained. "But he never had a parrot before."

A parrot? Nancy looked closer.

Perched on the pirate's shoulder was a green-and-red parrot!

"It's got to be Lester!" Katie cried.

The pirate stopped. He glanced over his other shoulder and raised his eye patch. Then he began to run!

"Stop!" Nancy called.

Could Captain Hook be the parrot crook?

4

Yo, Ho—Oh, No!

Why would a pirate want a parrot anyway?" Mari asked as they chased Captain Hook down the hall.

"So he can repeat directions to buried treasure!" George said. "Duh!"

Captain Hook's cape fluttered as he raced around a corner. The girls skidded around the corner, too.

Captain Hook glanced back before slipping through a door. The girls slowed down. Hanging on the door was a sign that read THE JOLLY JELLYFISH—DANGER!

"I don't like that word," Bess said.

"Me neither." Mari shivered. "I was once stung by a jellyfish."

"Not that!" Bess said. "I don't like the word *danger*!"

"Neither do I," Katie said. "But I have to get Lester back once and for all."

Katie pushed the door open. The girls peeked inside. When Nancy didn't see the pirate, she waved everyone into the room.

"Where are we?" Bess whispered.

Amara pointed to a big black and white flag hanging against a wall. "We're inside the *Jolly Jellyfish*," she declared.

Nancy knew it was just another room, but it really did look like a pirate ship.

Instead of windows there were portholes. Nets hung from the ceiling. Treasure maps were strewn over the floor. But there was no Captain Hook!

"Looks like the captain jumped ship," Amara said.

"Great," Mari muttered. "Now I'll never get his picture!"

"And I'll never get Lester!" Katie moaned.

"You guys!" George interrupted. "Check it out."

Nancy turned to George. She was dragging

a medium-size chest to the middle of the room. Nancy thought it looked like a treasure chest.

"It must be Captain Hook's treasure chest," Mari said.

"Don't open it!" Bess cried. "You know what Captain Hook did to Tiger Lily—he tied her up!"

"Bess, this is make believe," Amara said. "I . . . hope."

George lifted the lid. Nancy and her friends stared inside. It was filled with colorful plastic rings and bracelets!

"Awesome!" Mari cried. She slipped a bright green ring on her finger.

Amara pulled out a note and read it out loud: "Treasure your sleepover. Luv, Aunt Ellen!"

The girls had fun putting on the rings and bracelets.

"Purple and pink are my favorite colors!" Nancy exclaimed. "They match my—"

Creeeeeeak!

Nancy looked up. She saw a net sagging down from the ceiling.

The girls jumped up. It was too late. The

net fell down over all of them!

"We're trapped!" Bess cried, tearing at the net. "Get ready to walk the plank!"

Through the net Nancy saw Captain Hook—stepping out from behind the *Jolly Jellyfish* flag!

"Ahoy!" the pirate snarled. "Thought you could steal my swag, arrrgh?"

The parrot on his shoulder squawked. Its head spun around and around.

"Who's a pretty bird?" it squawked. "Who's a pretty bird? Arrrk!"

"Since when does Lester wear an eye patch?" George whispered under the net.

"He doesn't," Katie whispered. "And his head doesn't spin like that either!"

The pirate used his hook-hand to flick a switch on the wall. The net slowly began to rise.

When the girls were free, Nancy studied the parrot. It looked more like some kind of robot.

"That's not Lester," Nancy said. "That parrot isn't even real!"

"Neither is your jewelry!" the parrot joked. "Har, har, har! Arrrk!"

Captain Hook leaned over and whispered. "Aye—Sophie is mechanical," he said. "But don't let her hear that."

"Why?" Mari laughed. "Does she think she's a *real* parrot?"

"No," Captain Hook said. "A real chicken!"

"Cluck, cluck!" Sophie screeched.

Everyone giggled except Katie. Nancy couldn't blame her. The parrot she hoped was Lester was just a fake.

"You're not going to take our jewelry, are you?" Bess asked Captain Hook.

"Shiver me timbers!" The pirate laughed. He held up his hook-hand. "Does this look like a hand that wears rings?"

The girls giggled.

"Besides," Captain Hook said, "there's an old pirate saying about finding buried treas-arrrgh!"

"What?" Nancy asked.

The pirate kicked up his heels and began to dance. "Finders keepers losers weepers!" he sang. "Arrrgh!"

Nancy was happy that the pirate was nice. But she still had some questions.

"Captain Hook," she said, "do you know if

anyone in the house is doing weird things?"

"Everyone in this house is weird," Captain Hook answered. "What do you mean?"

Nancy was about to explain when— *Splash!* Water began gushing through the portholes into the room. And all over them!

"We're sailin' into a storm!" Captain Hook shouted. "Lower the sail! Close the cannon ports! Batten down the hatches!"

"You do that," George told the pirate. "I'm outta here!"

"Arrk! Cluck, cluck!" squawked Sophie.

Nancy's reddish blond bangs were soaked. She turned and reached for the doorknob. There she saw another spider!

What do all these spider stickers mean? Nancy wondered as they ran out.

Once in the hall, George turned to Amara. "Don't tell me, let me guess," she said. "That never happened before either."

"No," Amara said. "And if you ask me, Captain Hook looked pretty surprised, too."

Mari, George, and Katie sat on the staircase. Nancy, Amara, and Bess leaned on the banister.

"What do we do now?" Amara asked.

Nancy saw a phone hanging on the wall. It gave her an idea. "I know!" Nancy said. "I'll call my dad. He's a lawyer and he always helps me with my cases."

"Good idea," George said.

But when Nancy placed the receiver against her ear, she heard a strange, deep laugh: "Mwah, hah, hah, haaaa!"

Nancy gulped and hung up. "Or maybe I'll solve this case all by myself."

Katie slumped back on a stair. "I can't believe this is happening!" she said. "I can't believe Lester is missing!"

"Don't look now," George said. "But someone else is missing."

"Who?" Mari asked.

"Bess!" George replied.

"Bess?" Nancy gasped.

Her eyes darted around for her friend. George was right. Bess was gone!

5

Bubble Trouble

O h, great," Katie groaned. "First Lester—now Bess!"

"Or maybe Bess is playing a trick on us!" Mari said.

The girls ran up and down the hall calling Bess's name. They checked behind plants, doors, even behind a tall clock. But Bess was nowhere to be found!

"Poor Bess!" George cried. "I'll never call her clothes prissy again!"

"You promise?" a voice asked.

Nancy and her friends froze. The voice belonged to Bess!

"I think it came from around the corner!" Mari said.

The girls raced down the hall and skidded

around the corner. There Nancy saw Bess. She was standing in front of a door that was covered with candy bars and lollipops.

"I thought I smelled chocolate," Bess said, peeling off a chocolate-caramel bar. "But I never thought I'd find all this!"

"Why didn't you answer when we called your name?" George cried, waving her arms.

"My mouth was full," Bess said. She shrugged. "And it's not polite to speak with your mouth full."

George looked mad. "Be careful. Or you'll get chocolate all over your prissy clothes!" she snapped.

"George!" Bess said. "You promised!"

"Stop fighting," Nancy said. "The most important thing is that we found Bess."

"And all this candy!" Mari said. She took a quick picture. "Let's pig out!"

Nancy studied the candy-covered door. She had never seen anything like it.

"This is the door that leads to the witch's cottage," Amara explained.

"Which witch?" Mari asked.

"The witch from 'Hansel and Gretel,'" Amara said. "The one who Lester bit."

"Nipped!" Katie corrected.

"Uh-oh," Bess said. She dropped a purple lollipop. "When she finds out I was eating her candy—she'll bust a wart!"

"No!" Amara said, smiling. "She wants you to eat it. That's why it's there."

But Nancy was more interested in what was *behind* the door. She reached out and grabbed the doorknob.

"What are you doing?" Bess asked.

"The witch is a suspect," Nancy said. "She might be making all these weird things happen. And she might have Lester, too."

The door creaked as Nancy opened it. Slowly she peeked inside.

The room looked like the inside of a tiny cottage. The walls were made of stone. A big basket sat on a wooden table. There was a tall cabinet against one wall, and a big black pot against the other.

"Is the witch in there?" Mari hissed.

"No," Nancy said. "But let's go inside and look for clues."

The girls stepped into the room. Bess ran straight to the basket and looked inside.

"Cool!" Bess said. "It's filled with raisins, nuts, and dried fruit."

"That witch may be mean," Mari said, shaking her head, "but she sure knows how to throw a party."

"I don't think it's from the witch," Amara said. She opened a note next to the basket. "It's from my aunt Ellen!"

Nancy read the note over Amara's shoulder: "Sweets for a sweet sleepover! Luv, Aunt Ellen."

"Who wants dried apricots?" Bess asked, reaching into the basket.

"Who wants nuts?" George asked.

"All I want is Lester." Katie sighed sadly.

The treats looked yummy but Nancy wanted to look for more clues. She walked over to the cabinet and tried to open it. The door was locked.

Nancy was about to look for a key when she heard a strange gurgling noise.

"What's that sound?" Nancy asked.

Her friends stopped eating to listen.

"It can't be my stomach," Bess said. "It's too full."

Nancy followed the noise to the black

pot. Her mouth dropped open when she looked inside. The pot was filled with a thick, green, bubbling liquid!

The other girls ran to the pot, too.

"Yuck!" Bess said.

"What is it?" Katie asked.

"Well, it's not chicken soup!" George said.

"I know," Amara said. "It's the witch's brew. She always has something brewing in her cauldron."

Nancy looked at the brew through her magnifying glass. She saw something red floating on the top. "Does the recipe call for feathers?" she asked Amara.

Katie gripped the rim of the cauldron. "Feathers!" She gasped. "The witch said she needed them for her brew!"

Nancy reached for a broom. Using the handle she fished out the red feather.

"Say!" Mari said. "Doesn't Lester have—"

George nudged Mari but it was too late. Katie put the pieces together.

"Lester!" Katie cried. "He was my only pet. Now he's—*parrot chowder!*"

Gurgle, gurgle, gurgle!

The noise got louder and louder. Nancy

froze as the brew began bubbling faster and faster and faster!

"It's out of control!" Amara cried as the brew bubbled over the brim.

The girls shrieked and ran to the door. But when Nancy turned the doorknob, the door wouldn't budge.

Nancy looked over her shoulder. The brew was bubbling out of the cauldron and oozing across the floor.

"You guys," Amara said, "this has never happened—"

"We know, we know." George groaned.

Nancy tried turning the doorknob again. This time she felt someone opening it from the other side.

"Aunt Ellen?" Nancy called.

The door flew open and the girls jumped back. Standing in the doorway was the witch! And she had a big bandage on her nose!

6

Stairs to Where?

What are you doing in my cottage?" the witch demanded as she stepped inside.

But when she saw the bubbling brew her eyes popped wide open!

"Cheese and crackers!" the witch exclaimed. "How did that happen?"

"You mean you don't know?" Nancy asked.

The witch shook her head.

"I'll bet you know what happened to Lester!" Katie said bravely.

"Lester?" the witch cried. "You mean that bird who bit my honker?"

"Nipped!" Katie corrected.

"Do you know where he is?" Nancy asked the witch.

"I don't know what you're talking about," the witch said.

But Nancy wasn't finished asking questions.

"Can you tell us where you were in the last hour?" Nancy asked the witch.

The witch pointed to her bandaged nose. "After cracker-breath bit my nose, I went straight to the River Heights Hospital emergency room," she said.

"You were there all this time?" Nancy asked.

The witch nodded. "You should have seen all the people in the waiting room," she said. "But after I turned them into toads, the doctor took me right away."

Silence.

"Kidding!" the witch said.

Nancy believed the witch. Only a doctor could wrap such a big nose so neatly.

The cauldron finally stopped bubbling. Nancy remembered the feather.

"You said you needed a parrot feather for your brew," Nancy told the witch. "So what was a red feather doing inside your cauldron?"

The witch cackled.

She reached into the pocket of her apron and pulled out a key. She walked to the cabinet and unlocked it.

The witch pulled the door wide open. Inside the cupboard Nancy saw a feather duster. A big red feather duster!

"A feather must have fallen into the cauldron while I was dusting it!" the witch explained.

Nancy believed the witch again. The feather in the brew was the same color as the feathers on the duster.

The witch planted her hands on her hips. "Any other questions?" she asked.

"Just one," Mari said. "Is that nose of yours . . . for real?"

"What do you think it is, girlie?" the witch sneered. "A salami?"

"Lester must have thought so." Katie sighed. "He loves salami."

"Well, I hope you find your bird," the witch said. "If not, try dropping some bread crumbs. It worked for Hansel and Gretel."

The girls said good-bye to the witch and left the room. Nancy opened her notebook and crossed out the witch's name.

"Did you see how surprised she was when she saw the ooze?" Amara asked.

"Someone *is* doing weird things in this house," Nancy said. She checked out her suspect list. Her only two suspects were Ernest and the troll.

"Can we go to the library?" Katie asked. "Maybe Lester flew back to his cage in the meantime."

But when the girls returned to the library, Lester wasn't there. Instead there were two women in the middle of the room. One was tall. The other one was short.

"They're Cinderella's wicked stepsisters!" Amara said with a smile.

More villains! Nancy thought.

"So!" the short sister said. "Thought you could sneak off to the prince's ball?"

Nancy shook her head. "We were just looking for a parrot," she said.

"Next you'll be telling us you were looking for your glass slipper!" The tall sister laughed.

"You girls are not going anywhere until you clean this room!" the short one said.

Nancy glanced around the library. The books were back on the shelves. The pizza slices were back in the box.

"Clean what?" Nancy asked.

The sisters stepped aside. They pointed to a trail of white powdery footprints on the carpet.

"Ta-daa!" the tall one sang. She took a handful of brushes from a blue pail. She gave one to each of the girls. "Now stop gabbing and start scrubbing!"

The girls got down on their hands and knees. They began to brush the footprints.

"Smile," Amara whispered. "This is supposed to be funny."

"Ha, ha," George grumbled.

The footprints brushed off easily. When they were done the girls stood up.

Nancy folded her arms and leaned against the bookcase. Then something strange happened. She felt the bookcase move! Nancy stepped forward and the bookcase sprang back. Too weird!

"Nice job, girls," the tall sister said. "Those footprints are history!"

But they weren't history for long. After a

Nancy Drew . . . "Clues from the past. She
thinks that maybe the journal that's in our
store was written . . ."

few seconds the footprints began to reappear—one by one!

"Those are trick footprints right?" Bess asked.

"If it's a trick it's a good one," the tall sister gulped. "I've never seen that happen before."

"Me neither!" The short one said. "Forget about working overtime. I'm outta here!"

The stepsisters lifted the hems of their skirts and bolted out the door.

"Did you see how they flipped when those footprints came back?" George asked.

"Hey!" Bess called. She pointed into the blue bucket. "This bucket is filled with sheets of stickers. Glittery ones!"

"And here's a note from my aunt Ellen," Amara said. She pulled out a piece of paper. "It says: 'You glow, girls!'"

Nancy liked stickers. But she couldn't wait to show everyone what she found.

"Look everybody!" Nancy called. She gave the bookcase a push. This time it swung open like a door. A secret door!

"Neato-mosquito!" George exclaimed.

Everyone ran to look inside.

Nancy saw a staircase leading down-stairs. "Where does it lead, Amara?" she asked.

"Don't know." Amara shrugged. "I never saw this staircase in my life!"

"Then there's only one way to find out," Nancy said.

She took a deep breath. And she stepped through the secret door!

7

Tricky Troll

The girls filed down the stairs. At the bottom of the staircase was another door. Nancy opened it slowly.

"Where are we?" Nancy asked as they filed into a big room. It was filled with racks of costumes, cardboard trees and cottages— even a fake giant pumpkin!

"It's the storage room," Amara said. "So we must be in the basement."

"Neat!" Mari said. Her camera flashed as she took a picture of the pumpkin.

"Arrk!"

Nancy gasped. Lester was flapping out from behind the pumpkin!

"It's Lester!" Katie cried happily. "He was probably scared by the flash!"

"Good work, Mari!" Nancy exclaimed.

"Don't mention it," Mari said.

A small figure wearing a white beard and a red cap stumbled out after Lester.

"The troll!" Bess cried.

"Cotton candy! Raaak!" Lester squawked. He flapped onto the troll's shoulder and began tugging at his beard.

"Lester, stop!" Katie scolded.

Lester yanked the beard off. Nancy stared at the troll's face. But it wasn't the troll at all. It was Amara's little cousin Ernest!

"You!" Amara shouted.

"Busted." Ernest sighed.

"Why are you wearing the troll's costume, Ernest?" Amara demanded. "And tell us the truth—no fairy tales!"

"It wasn't my idea!" Ernest insisted. "Before you guys came to the house the troll asked me to wear it. So I said yes."

"You wanted to wear his costume?" Nancy asked.

"Sure!" Ernest said. "This way I could sneak around and snoop on your sleepover!"

The girls frowned at Ernest.

"But I didn't!" Ernest went on. "After I

saw Lester I had a better idea. I'd have my *own* sleepover—with Lester!"

"A sleepover with a parrot?" George asked.

"Sure," Ernest said. "But Lester wasn't a great guest. He kept trying to eat my beard."

"Cotton candy!" Lester screeched.

"So that's who was hiding behind the potted plant," Mari said. "It was Ernest!"

"He was waiting to sneak into the library so he could take Lester," Katie added.

"And he snuck out with Lester through the secret door!" Nancy exclaimed.

Ernest wrinkled his nose. "What are you all—detectives?" he cried.

"Just one of us is," Bess said, pointing to Nancy. "But we like to help."

Ernest heaved a big sigh. "I guess the door isn't a secret anymore," he said.

"And speaking of secrets," Nancy said. "Were you trying to scare us, too?"

Nancy mentioned the tumbling books, the fireplace, and the footprints.

"No way!" Ernest said. "The only trick I played was the rubber bat. I'm not allowed to go near the controls!"

Nancy studied Ernest. "Is he telling the truth?" she muttered to Amara.

"Yeah," Amara muttered back. "When Ernest lies his nose twitches. It's not twitching now."

Nancy believed that Ernest just wanted Lester. But now her only suspect was the troll.

"Tell us where the troll is," Nancy said to Ernest. "You've got to know."

"Can't," Ernest said. "I promised I wouldn't. And a promise is a promise."

"Okay," Amara said. "But wait till your mom finds out that you put that whoopie cushion on grandma's chair last Thanksgiving—"

"You said you wouldn't tell!" Ernest cried.

"But I never promised," Amara said with a wide grin.

"Okay, okay," Ernest said. "The troll is in my room. Check it out."

Amara led the girls out of the storage room and up to the third floor.

"This is it," Amara said. She pointed to a blue door.

"What if it's a trick?" Bess whispered. "What if he has a whole room full of rubber bats?"

"Or smelly socks!" Mari gasped.

Nancy pressed her ear against the door. She could hear a man's voice.

"Steal third!" he was saying. "What are you waiting for? Steal third!"

Nancy recognized the voice. It belonged to the troll.

Without knocking, Nancy pushed the door open. She saw a little man sitting on the floor. He was wearing a sweatshirt, jeans, and Ernest's baseball cap. He was staring at a round object in his lap.

"Looks like we got your goat," George growled. *"Troll!"*

Startled, the troll jumped. The glass object flew out of his hands and into Nancy's.

"What's this?" Nancy gasped.

"That's my aunt's crystal ball!" Amara explained. "But it's really a TV."

Nancy looked inside the TV crystal-ball. There was a baseball game going on!

"Rats!" the troll muttered. "They were just in the bottom of the seventh!"

"So that's the plan you had up your sleeve," Nancy said. "Ernest would wear your costume while you hid in his room and watched the baseball game."

"You got me," the troll admitted.

"That was sneaky!" Amara scolded. "You were supposed to be working tonight."

The troll looked worried. "Are you going to tell your aunt Ellen?" he asked.

"I don't have to tell her," Amara said. She nodded at Mari. "I'll *show* her!"

Mari snapped a picture of the troll.

"Hey!" the troll cried. "Now your aunt will see me without my costume!"

"Exactly!" Mari said.

"And if that doesn't work," Katie said, smiling. "Lester has a *big* mouth!"

"Steal third! Steal third!" Lester squawked. "Arrrk!"

"Give me a break!" the troll groaned.

"But we won't tell if you get back to work," Amara said firmly.

"Okay, okay." The troll sighed. "Our team is losing anyway."

The girls left the troll in Ernest's room. Nancy handed Amara the crystal ball. Then she crossed Ernest's and the troll's name off her suspect list.

"So if it's not the witch, or Ernest, or the troll," Bess said, "who *is* making all those weird things happen?"

Nancy didn't know. But she knew they had to return Aunt Ellen's crystal ball.

"Let's put the crystal ball in Aunt Ellen's office," Nancy said. "If she's there we'll tell her the troll found it."

This time the girls didn't take the secret staircase. They climbed the usual stairs all the way up to the tower.

"Isn't it strange," Nancy told her friends, "that every time something weird happens, something nice happens, too?"

"Like the cookies, the sweets, and the stickers," Bess pointed out.

"Those were from my aunt Ellen," Amara said, a bit angrily. "Are you saying that my aunt is trying to scare us?"

"No," Nancy said. She didn't want Amara to be mad. "It was just a thought."

When the girls reached the tower it was empty. Amara placed the crystal ball on Aunt Ellen's desk.

"Let's leave her a note that we returned it," Nancy said.

She sifted through the papers on the desk for a notepad. Her eyes fell on a bright red folder with a silver design.

Nancy picked up the folder and studied it. The design was a spider!

Taking out her notebook, Nancy compared her sketch of the spider stickers she kept finding around the house with the one on the folder. They matched!

"Look!" Nancy cried. "It's the exact same spider that's all over the house!"

8

Party On!

Why is the spider on the folder?" Amara asked, wrinkling her brow.

Nancy opened the folder. The papers inside all had a silver spider in the top corner. And the words: "Slinky Spider Special Effects Company."

"What are special effects?" Mari asked, looking over Nancy's shoulder.

Nancy knew. She had seen a show about special effects on TV.

"Special effects make weird things look real," Nancy explained. "Like people flying and animals talking in the movies."

"You mean like magic?" Bess asked.

"Sort of," Nancy said. She pulled out the next page. It was a list of special effects—

an overflowing cauldron, squirting port-holes, a cracking mirror!

Nancy read each one out loud.

"So that's it," George said. "It was the Slinky Spider Company that made all those things happen."

"And they left silver spider stickers to sign their work!" Nancy decided.

Bess sighed with relief. "So the house *isn't* spooked!" she said.

"And my aunt Ellen planned the whole thing," Amara said. She turned to Nancy. "I'm sorry I acted mad. But why didn't my aunt tell us in the first place?"

"I don't know," Nancy said. "Why don't we ask her?"

Nancy put the folder under her arm. Then she and her friends left the tower.

They searched the rooms on the second floor. No Aunt Ellen. As they climbed down to the main floor they called Aunt Ellen's name. No answer.

"Now, where did she go?" Amara asked on the staircase.

Nancy heard footsteps. She looked down and saw a flash of red running down the hall. The person wore a red cape, a red hood, and Mary Jane shoes. She carried a basket over her arm.

"It looks like Little Red Riding Hood!" Nancy said, racing down the stairs.

"Little Red Riding Hood?" Bess asked. "She's not a villain!"

"Raaak!" Lester screeched. He flew off of Katie's shoulder and toward the figure in red.

"Lester!" Katie shouted. "Come back!"

Lester landed on top of the red hood and it dropped down.

"Hey! That's not Little Red Riding Hood!" Amara cried. "It's my aunt Ellen!"

With Lester perched on her head, Aunt Ellen walked over. She held up the basket.

"I was going to leave these donuts for you in the wolf's cottage," Aunt Ellen said. "But you caught me jelly-handed!"

Nancy peeked inside. The basket was filled with yummy-looking jelly donuts.

"Thanks for the neat surprises, Aunt Ellen," Nancy said. "But there were lots of other surprises we didn't expect."

"Oh?" Aunt Ellen asked. Her eyes twinkled. "Like what?"

Nancy told Aunt Ellen about the bubbling cauldron, the cracked mirror, the squirting portholes. . . .

"And," Nancy went on, "the little silver spider."

"What spider?" Aunt Ellen asked.

Nancy held up the folder. "The *Slinky Spider*!" she replied.

Aunt Ellen stared at the folder. Then she threw back her head and laughed.

"Whoops!" Aunt Ellen said. "I guess the cat is out of the bag!"

She put two fingers in her mouth and gave a shrill whistle. All the doors opened. Curious villains peeked out.

"Meeting in the library now!" Aunt Ellen hollered. "Be there!"

The girls followed the witch, the goats, the pirate, and the troll into the library.

"Psst," the troll whispered. "You didn't rat on me, did you?"

"Don't worry," Nancy whispered back. "Your secret is safe with us."

Nancy giggled to herself. The troll was in his costume—but forgot to change his sneakers!

When everyone was inside the library Aunt Ellen began to speak.

"I was the one who planned all those strange effects," she announced.

"Why didn't you tell us?" Amara asked.

Aunt Ellen smiled at Amara.

"I did it for you, Amara," she said. "You knew this house so well. So I wanted to really surprise you and your friends."

"Shiver me timbers!" the pirate exclaimed. He waved his hook hand. "She wasn't the only one who was surprised!"

"I wanted *everyone* to be surprised," Aunt Ellen said. "That's why I gave you two weeks off last month. So you wouldn't see the Slinky Spider Company at work."

"Did Ernest know?" Amara asked.

"Ernest was the only one who knew my plans," Aunt Ellen said. She looked around. "By the way. Where is Ernest?"

One of the bookcases began to move. The secret door opened and Ernest stepped out. He was wearing his baseball cap—and the troll's shoes.

"What's up?" Ernest asked cheerily.

Aunt Ellen turned to the girls. "I hope you weren't too scared."

"If we weren't," Nancy said with a smile, "it wouldn't be Scarytales!"

"And we still had a blast!" George admitted.

"Well, the fun has just begun," Aunt Ellen declared. "The villains have agreed to work overtime so we can party on!"

"Yaaay!" the girls cheered.

Nancy had a lot to cheer about. She had solved another case. And there was still plenty of time for sleepover fun.

The girls bobbed for apples in the witch's cauldron. They learned pirate songs from Captain Hook. They even posed for Mari's camera in fairy-tale costumes.

But when the clock struck midnight, Nancy and her friends began to yawn.

"So much for staying up all night," George said after they changed into their pajamas and snuggled into their sleeping bags.

"I can't believe we made friends with a troll, a pirate—even a witch!" Bess said with a yawn.

"And look!" Katie said, pointing. "Lester made a new friend, too."

Nancy looked to see where Katie was pointing. Perched on the mantel were Lester and the mechanical parrot, Sophie.

"Who's a pretty bird?" Lester squawked. "Arrrk!"

Nancy laughed. But when she glanced back at her friends they were all asleep!

Nancy was sleepy too, but she had work to do. She took out her notebook and opened it to a clean page. Then by the light of an electric jack-o'-lantern, she began to write. . . .

Amara's sleepover was a big success! And Katie has Lester back, too. Okay . . . I was a little scared. But in the end we all lived happily ever after.

And that's what really counts!

CASE CLOSED!

THE UNICORN'S SECRET

Experience the Magic

When the battered mare Heart Trilby takes in presents her with a silvery white foal, Heart's life is transformed into one of danger, wonder, and miracles beyond her wildest imaginings. Read about Heart's thrilling quest in

THE UNICORN'S SECRET # ① :
Moonsilver
0-689-84269-4

THE UNICORN'S SECRET # ② :
The Silver Thread
0-689-84270-8

THE UNICORN'S SECRET # ③ :
The Silver Bracelet
0-689-84271-6

THE UNICORN'S SECRET # ④ :
The Mountains of the Moon
0-689-84272-4

ALADDIN PAPERBACKS
Simon & Schuster Children's Publishing Division • www.SimonSaysKids.com